Here comes spring

and summer and autumn and winter

Mary Murphy

Here comes spring!

The apple blossom

flies in the breeze.

We do some work
in the garden.

I meet my
friend in
the park.

In summer we have picnics.

The sun is high in the sky.

We rest in the shade.

and ready to pick.

The wind messes
up the garden.

In winter the birds are hungry.

We have a snow fight.

Look at our snowdog!

Night comes early.

To my mother, Anna Murphy

A DORLING KINDERSLEY BOOK

First published in Great Britain in 1999 by Dorling Kindersley Limited,
9 Henrietta Street, London WC2E 8PS

Visit us on the World Wide Web at http://www.dk.com

A CIP catalogue record for this book is available from the British Library.

ISBN 0-7513-7164-5

Colour Reproduction by DOT Gradations

Printed in Singapore by Tien Wah Press